A los niños de El Salvador
To the children of El Salvador
—Manlio Argueta

*Dedicated to the children of all the Americas and to all the magical cadejo/coyote/trickster
dogs in my life! Many thanks to Veg, Armagh and Harriet for being great work partners
in this endeavor; and to John for being the supportive honey that he is!
—Elly Simmons*

Story copyright © 1990 by Manlio Argueta and Stacey Ross
Pictures copyright © 1990 by Elly Simmons

Editors: Harriet Rohmer and David Schecter
Spanish language consultant: Rosalma Zubizarreta
Design: Armagh Cassil and Mira Reisberg, Somar Graphics
Production Assistant: Julie Weigel
Typography: Berna Alvarado-Rodriguez
Printed in Hong Kong through Marwin Productions

Children's Book Press is a nonprofit community publisher. For a free catalog, write to:
Children's Book Press, 2211 Mission Street, San Francisco, CA 94110
Visit our website at www.childrensbookpress.org.

Publication of this book is supported in part by a grant from the National Endowment for the Arts.

Distributed to the book trade by Publishers Group West.
Quantity discounts available through the publisher for educational and nonprofit use.

Library of Congress Cataloging-in-Publication Data
Argueta, Manlio, 1936—
   Magic dogs of the volcanoes / story by Manlio Argueta with Stacey Ross, Harriet Rohmer & David Schecter; English translation by
Stacey Ross; pictures by Elly Simmons = Los perros mágicos de los volcanes / escrito por Manlio Argueta con la colaboración de Stacey
Ross, Harriet Rohmer & David Schecter; traducido al inglés por Stacey Ross; ilustrado por Elly Simmons.
      p. cm.
   English and Spanish.
   Summary: When the magic dogs who live on the volcanoes of El Salvador and protect the villagers from harm are pursued by wicked
lead soldiers, they are aided by two ancient volcanoes.
   ISBN 0-89239-129-4
   [1. El Salvador—Fiction. 2. Volcanoes—Fiction. 3. Dogs—Fiction. 4. Spanish language materials—Bilingual.] I. Simmons, Elly, ill.
II. Title. III. Title: Perros mágicos de los volcanes.
PZ73.A66   1990
[Fic]—dc20   90-2254
                                                                                                      CIP

MAGIC DOGS
OF THE VOLCANOES

LOS PERROS MÁGICOS DE LOS VOLCANES

Story by / Escrito por Manlio Argueta
Pictures by / Ilustrado por Elly Simmons
English translation by / Traducido al inglés por Stacey Ross

CHILDREN'S BOOK PRESS • SAN FRANCISCO, CALIFORNIA

On the volcanoes of El Salvador live magic dogs called cadejos. They look a lot like wolves, but they're not wolves. They move with the grace of deer, but they're not deer. They eat the seeds of the morning glories, those beautiful flowers that cover the volcanoes and look like little bells.

cadejos is pronounced: cah-dáy-hose

En los volcanes de El Salvador habitan
perros mágicos que se llaman cadejos. Se
parecen a los lobos aunque no son lobos. Y tienen
el garbo de venados aunque no son venados. Se alimentan
de las semillitas que echan las campánulas, esas lindas
flores que cubren los volcanes y que parecen campanitas.

The people who live in the villages on the slopes of the volcanoes have always loved the cadejos. They say the cadejos are really the great-great-grandchildren of the volcanoes. They say the cadejos have always protected them from danger and misfortune.

La gente que vive en las faldas de los volcanes quieren mucho a los cadejos. Dicen que los cadejos son los tataranietos de los volcanes y que siempre han protegido a la gente del peligro y de la desgracia.

When the people of the volcanoes travel from one village to another, a cadejo always goes along. If a child is in danger of stepping on a snake or falling in a hole, the cadejo will turn itself into a gust of wind and lift the child out of harm's way.

Cuando la gente de los volcanes viaja de un pueblo a otro, siempre hay un cadejo que las acompaña. Si un cipote está por pisar una culebra o caerse en un agujero, el cadejo se convierte en un soplo de viento que lo desvía del mal paso.

If an old man becomes very tired working under the hot sun, a cadejo will carry him to the shade of a nearby tree. The people of the volcanoes say they could not have survived to this day without the cadejos.

But sadly, not everybody has always loved the cadejos. No. Don Tonio and his 13 brothers who owned the land on the volcanoes did not like the cadejos at all.

Si un anciano se cansa de tanto trabajar bajo el sol ardiente, un cadejo lo transporta a la sombra de un árbol cercano. Por todo esto, la gente de los volcanes dice que, si no fuera por la ayuda de los cadejos, no hubieran podido sobrevivir hasta hoy en día.

Pero lamentablemente, no todos han querido siempre a los cadejos. ¡Qué va! A don Tonio y a sus trece hermanos, que eran los dueños de la tierra de los volcanes, no les gustaban los cadejos para nada.

The cadejos bewitch the people and make them lazy!"
Don Tonio said one day to his 13 brothers.

And Don Tonio's brothers answered: "Yes, it is true.
The people don't work hard for us anymore. They want
to eat when they are hungry and drink water when they
are thirsty and rest in the shade when the sun is hot.
And it's all because of the cadejos."

Los cadejos hechizan a la gente y la hacen perezosa!
—dijo un día don Tonio a sus hermanos.

Y los trece hermanos de don Tonio contestaron: —Sí, es
cierto. La gente ya no quiere trabajar duro para nosotros.
Quieren comer cuando tienen hambre. Quieren beber
cuando tienen sed. Quieren descansar bajo la sombra de
un árbol cuando arde el sol. ¡Y todo eso por los cadejos!

So Don Tonio and his 13 brothers called in the lead soldiers to go up on the volcanoes and hunt the cadejos. The lead soldiers set out with their tents and their canteens and their shining guns. "We will be the handsomest and most respected lead soldiers in the world," they said.

Entonces, don Tonio y sus trece hermanos llamaron a los soldados de plomo y los mandaron para los volcanes a cazar cadejos. Los soldados se pusieron en camino con sus tiendas de campaña, sus cantimploras y sus armas centellantes. —Vamos a ser los soldados de plomo más bellos y más respetados del mundo —se dijeron.

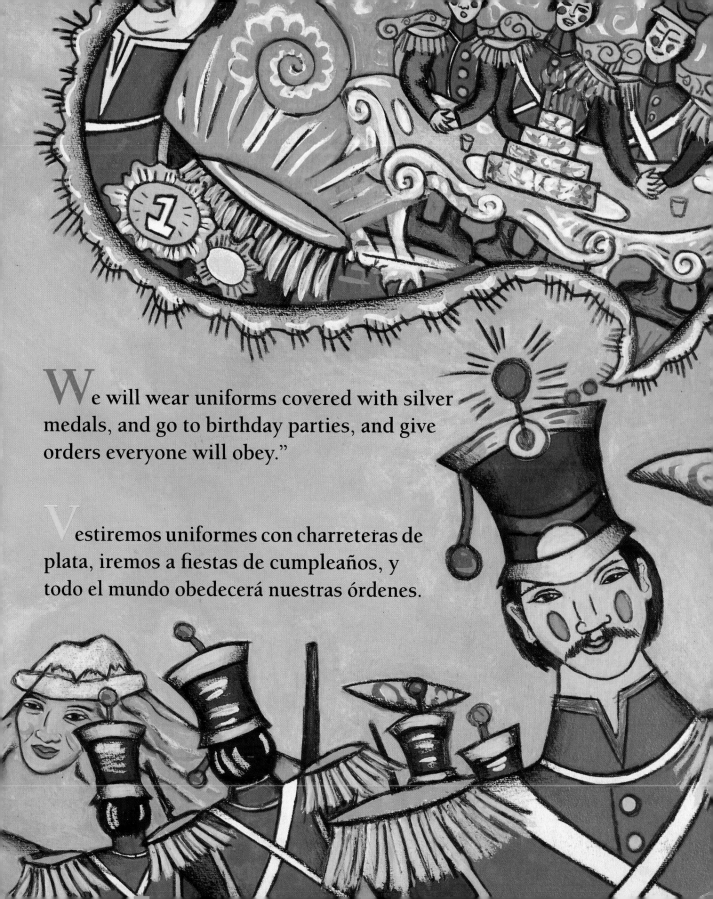

We will wear uniforms covered with silver medals, and go to birthday parties, and give orders everyone will obey."

Vestiremos uniformes con charreteras de plata, iremos a fiestas de cumpleaños, y todo el mundo obedecerá nuestras órdenes.

The lead soldiers marched toward the volcano Tecapa, who is a beautiful woman dressed in a robe of water and a hat of clouds. They marched toward the handsome volcano Chaparrastique with his hat of hot, white smoke.

Los soldados de plomo marcharon hacia el volcán Tecapa, que es mujer y viste un ropaje espléndido de agua y un sombrero de nubes. Y marcharon hacia Chaparrastique, un volcán hermoso que lleva siempre su sombrero blanco de humo caliente.

Chaparrastique is pronounced:
Chop-ah-ras-tée-kay

Let's hunt the cadejos while they sleep," said the lead soldiers. "That way we can take them by surprise with no danger to us."

They didn't know that the cadejos can put on garments of air and light that make them invisible. The lead soldiers searched and searched, but they couldn't find a single cadejo.

Cazaremos a los cadejos mientras duermen —dijeron los soldados de plomo—. Así podremos tomarlos desprevenidos sin correr ningún riesgo.

Pero no sabían que los cadejos visten un traje de luz de día y de aire, con lo cual se hacen transparentes. Los soldados de plomo busca que busca a los cadejos, pero no encontraban a ninguno.

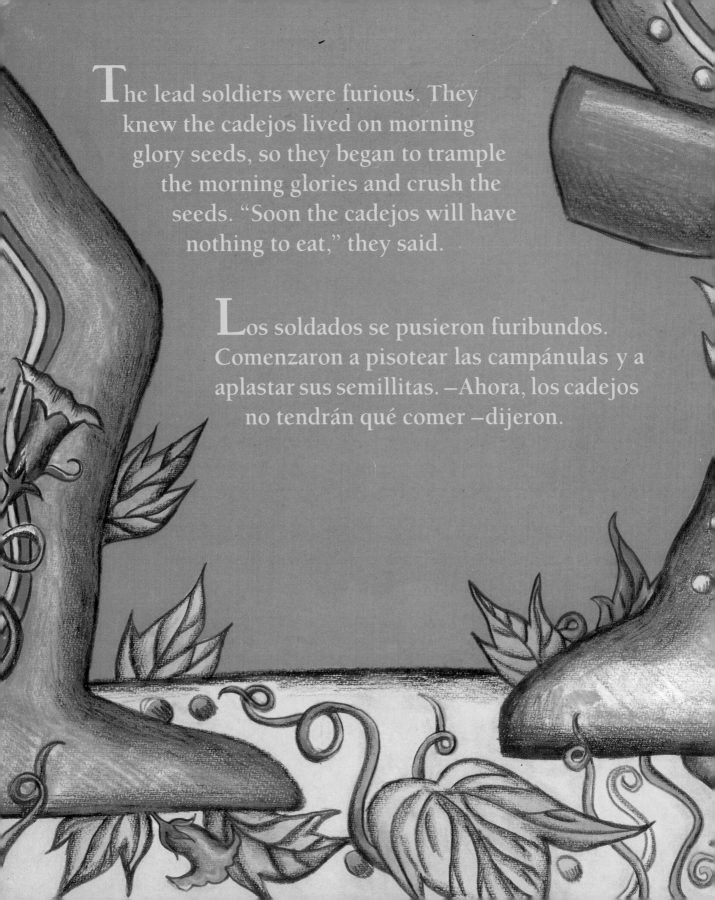

The lead soldiers were furious. They knew the cadejos lived on morning glory seeds, so they began to trample the morning glories and crush the seeds. "Soon the cadejos will have nothing to eat," they said.

Los soldados se pusieron furibundos. Comenzaron a pisotear las campánulas y a aplastar sus semillitas. —Ahora, los cadejos no tendrán qué comer —dijeron.

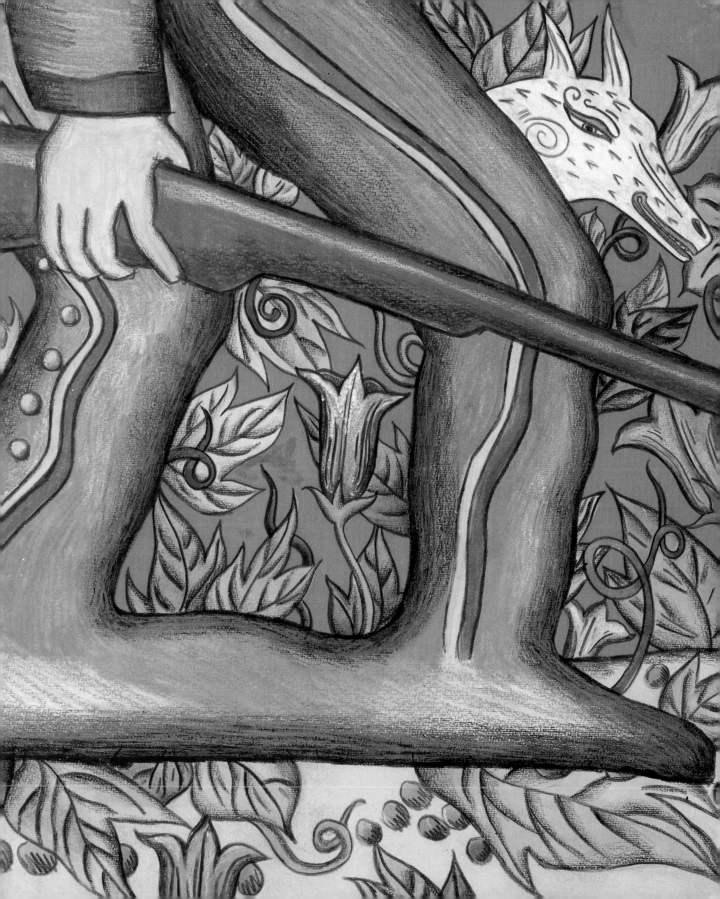

Never had the cadejos been in such danger. So they went for help to their great-great-grandparents, the volcanoes Tecapa and Chaparrastique. All night long the cadejos spoke with the volcanoes. Finally, Tecapa said, "The soldiers are made of lead, you say. Are their hearts and brains also made of lead?"

"Yes," answered the cadejos. "Even their feet are made of lead."

"Then I have a plan," said Tecapa.

Los cadejos nunca habían corrido tanto peligro. Así es que buscaron la ayuda de los tatarabuelos, los volcanes Tecapa y Chaparrastique. Toda la noche los cadejos hablaron con los volcanes hasta que comentó Tecapa: —Dicen ustedes que son soldados de plomo. ¿El corazón y el cerebro son de plomo también?

—¡Sí! —respondieron los cadejos—. ¡Hasta sus pies están hechos de plomo!

—Entonces, ¡ya está! —dijo Tecapa.

Tecapa spoke to Chaparrastique. "You have a steam hat and I have a dress made of water," she said. "You'll simply fan yourself with your hat until the ground gets hot and then I will shake my dress." Tecapa gave her dress a shake.

"What good will that do?" asked the cadejos.

"Just wait and see," answered Tecapa.

Y Tecapa le dijo a Chaparrastique: —Mira, como yo tengo vestido de agua y vos tenés sombrero de fumarolas, simplemente comenzás a abanicarte con el sombrero por todo tu cuerpo hasta que se caliente la tierra y entonces yo comienzo a sacudirme mi vestido de agua.

Y Tecapa se lo sacudió.

—Y eso, ¿qué daño les puede hacer? —preguntaron los cadejos.

—Bueno —dijo Tecapa—, probemos y ya veremos.

The next day as the lead soldiers climbed the volcanoes, Chaparrastique took off his hat and began to fan himself until it got so hot even he couldn't stand it.

At first the soldiers only felt a tingling in their feet, but soon their feet began to melt. Then, Tecapa shook her dress and got the soldiers wet. Their bodies began to sizzle like water on a hot iron.

Al día siguiente, cuando los soldados de plomo venían subiendo los volcanes, comenzó el Chaparrastique a quitarse el sombrero de fumarolas y a soplar sobre todo su cuerpo, hasta que ni él mismo aguantaba el calor.

Al principio, los soldados sentían sólo una picazón, pero al ratito los pies se les comenzaron a derretir. Entonces, Tecapa se sacudió el vestido y empezó a remojarles. Y los cuerpos de los soldados de plomo chirriaban, como cuando se le echa agua a una plancha caliente.

The lead soldiers felt very bad when they saw that their feet were melting. They sat down on the rocks to cry, but the rocks were so hot that their bottoms began to melt.

That is how the lead soldiers realized they couldn't defeat the cadejos, nor trample the morning glories, nor go up on the volcanoes with evil plans. They saw that being made of lead was a weakness and decided to devote themselves to professions more worthy than soldiering.

Los soldados de plomo se sentían muy mal y se sentaron a llorar sobre las piedras. Pero éstas estaban tan calientes que se les derretían las nalgas.

Fue así que los soldados de plomo se dieron cuenta que no era posible derrotar a los cadejos, ni pisotear a las campánulas, y, en fin, ni subir a los volcanes a hacer el mal. Y sabiendo que tenían la debilidad de estar hechos de plomo, lo mejor era cambiar de oficio y dedicarse a cosas más dignas.

From that day on there has been peace on the volcanoes of El Salvador. Don Tonio and his brothers ran away to other lands, while the cadejos and the people of the villages held a big party which was later remembered as a national holiday.

Desde entonces hay paz en los volcanes de El Salvador. Don Tonio y sus hermanos huyeron a otras tierras, mientras que los cadejos y la gente de los volcanes celebraron una gran fiesta que se convirtió en una inmensa fiesta nacional.

MAGIC DOGS OF THE VOLCANOES

Whenever Salvadoran people gather to tell stories, someone will have a story about the magic dogs called cadejos. There are many stories about how the cadejos mysteriously appear at night to protect people from danger. MAGIC DOGS OF THE VOLCANOES is Manlio Argueta's original story about these famous folkloric animals.

Manlio Argueta is one of El Salvador's greatest living authors. In 1977 he received Latin America's most prestigious literary award, the Casa de las Americas Prize, for *Caperucita en la Zona Roja*. He is also the author of *One Day of Life* (Vintage/Random House: 1983) and *Cuzcatlan Where the Southern Sea Beats* (Vintage/Random House: 1987). Argueta makes his home in San Jose, Costa Rica and travels frequently throughout the Americas. This is his first book for children. Stacey Ross is a California-based editor and translator.

Elly Simmons is a nationally-exhibited painter who has been actively involved in community and world issues for most of her life. She used watercolor, gouache, pastel and colored pencil on rag paper to produce the pictures for MAGIC DOGS OF THE VOLCANOES, her first book for children. Simmons lives in Lagunitas, California.